A is for Aspen
Text copyright 2012 by Maria Kernahan
Illustrations copyright 2012 by Michael Schafbuch

Printed in the United States

All rights reserved. For information about reproducing
selections from this book contact
Dry Climate Studios
www.dryclimatestudios.com

ISBN
978-0-9856429-0-7

Library of Congress Control Number: 2013946971

A is for Aspen

Written by Maria Kernahan

Illustrated by Michael Schafbuch

A is for aspen, the trees on the hill.
They stand together in groves so they don't get a chill.

B is for Buttermilk, a mountain for shredders.
It's got a big pipe - just don't take a header.

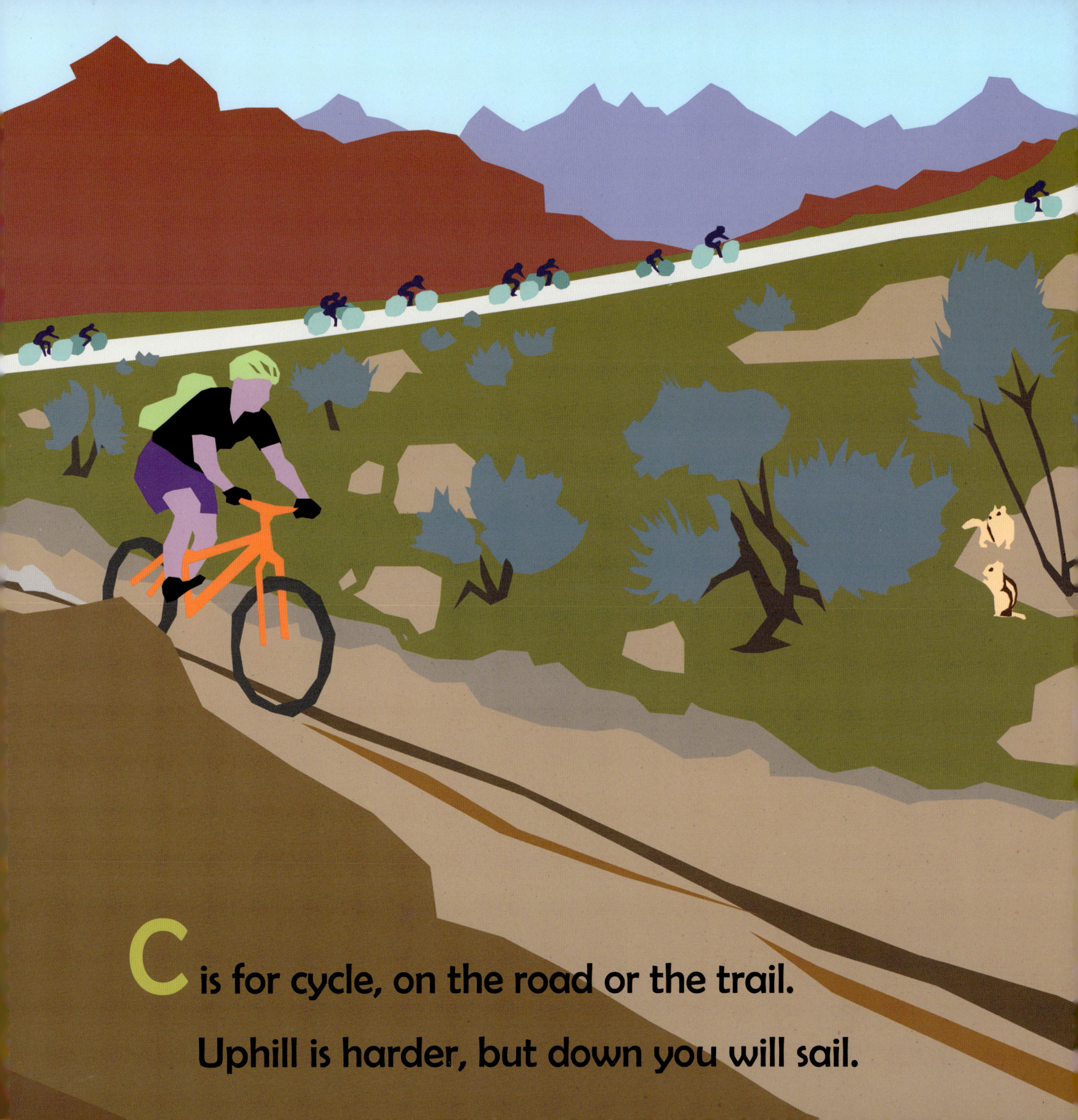

Once you start down you can never go back.

E is for elk, majestic and regal.
They migrate in June and are friends with the eagles.

F is for fly fishing, up here it's for trout.
Put on your big waders and throw your line out.

G is for gondola, it takes you up high.

H is for Highlands, with its Loges Peak lift.
The views of the Bells are truly a gift.

I is for Isis, the old movie house.

Grab a bucket of popcorn but be quiet as a mouse.

J is for Jerome, the hotel on Main.
It's been here forever and still looks the same.

K is for Krabloonik, the dog sledding place.

Hitch up the huskies and go for a race.

L is for Little Nell, the last run into town.
Named after a silver mine
now it's where you ski down.

M is for Music Festival under the tent.
All summer long it's a classical event.

N for Nastar, the big downhill race.
Slalom down the course and they'll time your pace.

O is for opera house,
the Wheeler is grand.

P is for prospectors who used trams with their mines.

They look like our chairlifts, with those pulleys and lines.

Q is for quad, the lift that takes four.

It gets you up fast so you can ski more.

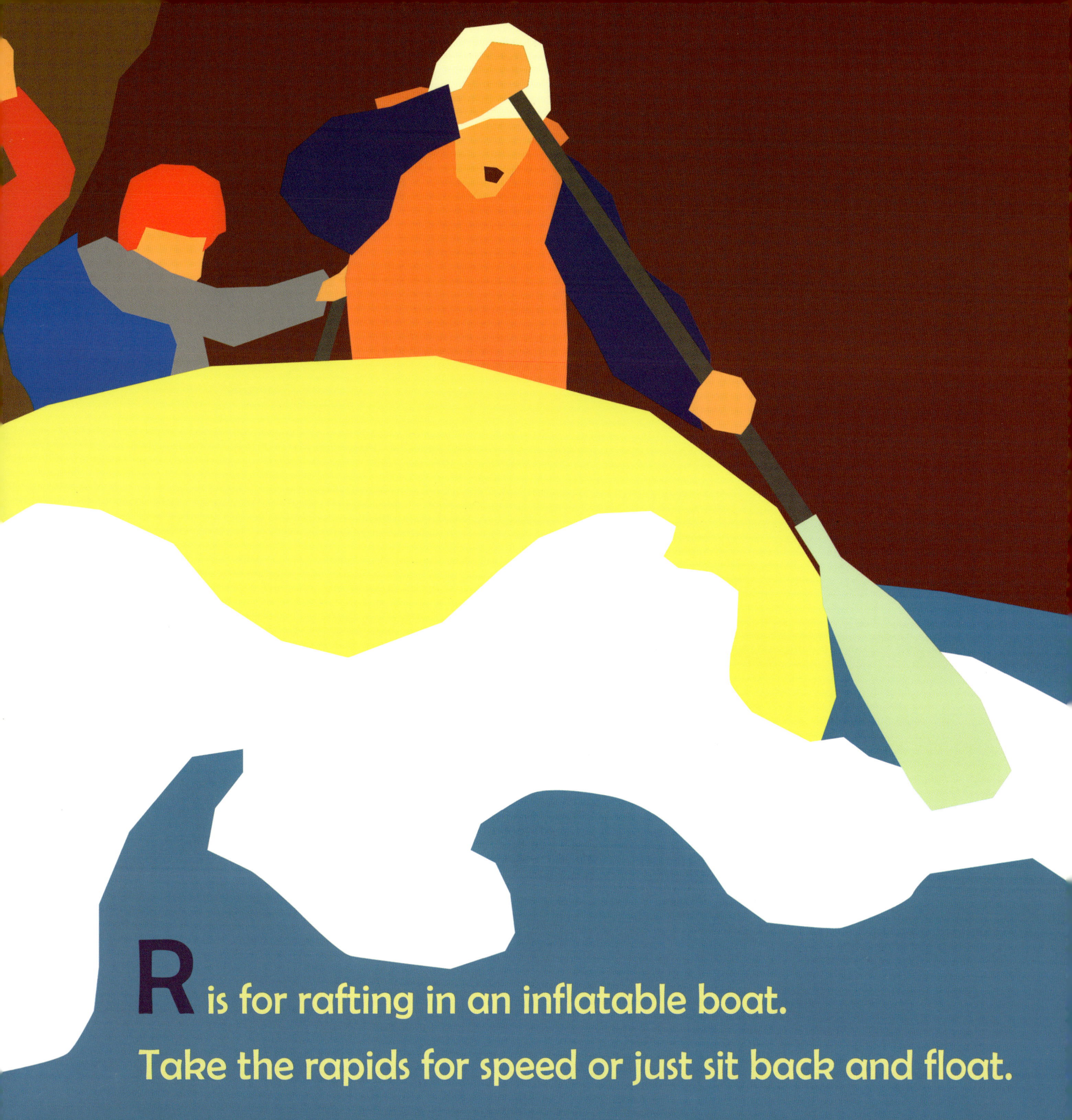

R is for rafting in an inflatable boat.
Take the rapids for speed or just sit back and float.

T is for tenth, the Tenth Mountain Division. They were WWII soldiers who skied with precision.

U is for Ute, Aspen's drum and song.

The bear is awake after sleeping so long.

V is for valley, Roaring Fork is its name.

Its the prettiest in Colorado, just part of its fame.

W is for Wintersköl, Aspen's Nordic fest.

It's a midwinter party that's really the best.

X is for X-Games, the extreme sport affair.

It has flips, jumps and races and lots of big air.